DREAMWORKS
HOW TO TRAIN YOUR
DRAGON 2

All About the
Dragons

by Judy Katschke

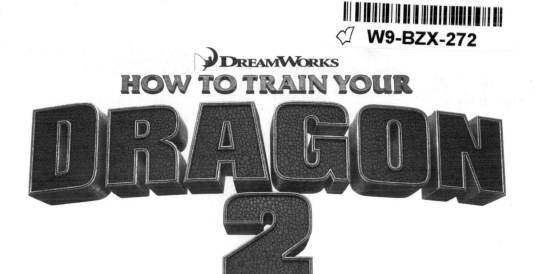

Ready-to-Read

Simon Spotlight

New York London Toronto Sydney New Delhi

SIMON SPOTLIGHT
An imprint of Simon & Schuster Children's Publishing Division
1230 Avenue of the Americas, New York, New York 10020
How To Train Your Dragon 2 © 2014 DreamWorks Animation L.L.C.
SIMON SPOTLIGHT, READY-TO-READ, and colophon are registered trademarks of
Simon & Schuster, Inc. For information about special discounts for bulk purchases, please contact
Simon & Schuster Special Sales at 1-866-506-1949 or business@simonandschuster.com.
The Simon & Schuster Speakers Bureau can bring authors to your live event. For more information
or to book an event contact the Simon & Schuster Speakers Bureau at 1-866-248-3049 or visit our
website at www.simonspeakers.com.
Manufactured in the United States of America 0614 LAK
6 8 10 9 7 5
ISBN 978-1-4814-0485-3 (pbk)
ISBN 978-1-4814-0486-0 (hc)
ISBN 978-1-4814-0487-7 (eBook)

Hiccup and his dragon, Toothless,
love exploring new worlds
and making new friends.
Many of their friends are dragons,
just like Toothless!

Toothless is a Night Fury,
an awesome kind of dragon!
Like all Night Furies,
he is very smart.
His sleek body is darker
than midnight.

His eyes glow in the dark
just like a cat's eyes.
Massive wings help him
soar through the sky.
He can even hide his teeth.
That is why he is called Toothless!

Meet Stormfly, a Deadly Nadder.
When Astrid rides Stormfly,
the patterns and colors
on the dragon's wings
brighten the sky.

But don't be fooled by her beauty.
When Stormfly is mad,
she shoots spines!

Stormfly is a steady flyer.
Astrid can walk on her back
while they are flying.
Now that's teamwork!

Like all Gronckles,
Meatlug's favorite food is rocks.
Her favorite hobby is sleeping!
Meatlug can sleep anywhere,
even in the sky!

But her favorite thing of all
is her favorite person, Fishlegs.
Meatlug loves licking his
feet every night . . .
and getting awesome belly rubs!

Not only does Hookfang breathe fire,
but he can also set himself on fire
when he needs protection!
It's no wonder he's called
a Monstrous Nightmare.

Hookfang has gigantic wings,
piercing fangs, and pointed claws.
When Hookfang races
with Snotlout, they often win.
This Monstrous Nightmare
is a Viking's dream come true!

The Hideous Zippleback is
two of a kind.
That's because it has two heads!
One head is named Barf.
The other is named Belch.

Like their riders,
Ruffnut and Tuffnut,
Barf and Belch have
minds of their own.
Barf spews gas. Belch sparks fire.
But together, Barf and Belch
always have a blast!

Seashockers are giant dragons
that live in the deep sea.
They have blades on their backs
that cut through the ocean.
They swim in pods,
like dolphins!

This is Cloudjumper.
He is a Stormcutter dragon.
When he flies, his wings are shaped
like the letter X!

Cloudjumper and his rider
take Hiccup and Toothless to their
home at Dragon Mountain.
The dragons and riders soon
become friends.

On Dragon Mountain,
Hiccup looks around.
He can't believe his eyes.
There are many
different kinds of dragons!
He has never seen
some of them before.

There is a Snaptrapper dragon
with four heads on its body!
Each of the four heads has jaws
that split three ways to trap prey.
There is also a Timberjack.
It has wide, razor-sharp wings
that can slice through the air!

Then Hiccup sees a
Thunderdrum dragon.
Its roar is like a sonic blast!
There is even a
Whispering Death dragon.

Its teeth are as sharp as needles!
It uses them to grind through dirt
and burrow underground,
making a whispering sound.

Hiccup soon meets the king
of Dragon Mountain,
the Bewilderbeast.
He is large and in charge.

His breath is icy cold,
and his roar is as loud as thunder.
All of the dragons on the mountain
obey his command.
Well, almost all the dragons. . . .

Baby dragon hatchlings are so young that they listen to no one! They don't even listen to the Bewilderbeast.

Hatchlings might be smaller
than adult dragons,
but they are big enough to ride!

Another Bewilderbeast belongs to a dragon thief named Drago Bludvist. His Bewilderbeast is trained to be bad, just like him!

When the two Bewilderbeasts
battle for power,
the bad dragon wins.
But the fight isn't over yet.

With a mighty roar,
Toothless defeats
the evil Bewilderbeast and Drago.
Hiccup cheers as the dragons
bow to their brave new leader.
Their new king is Toothless!

Toothless is now a hero
with more dragon friends than ever!
But his best friend doesn't
breathe fire or have wings.
His best friend isn't a dragon.
It's a Viking named Hiccup,
a dragon's friend for life!